Rom

The quaint, small town of Capeside, Massachusetts is not as quiet as one might think. Everyone is obsessing on the trials and tribulations of one particular group of fifteen-year-olds on the brink of adulthood. Find out all about the beautiful new megastars who have turned *Dawson's Creek* into the hottest show around.

Starring
James Van Der Beek as Dawson
Katie Holmes as Joey
Michelle Williams as Jen
Joshua Jackson as Pacey

The Stars of

DAWSON'S CREEK

by Hilary Rice

Infinity Plus One
Ridgewood, New Jersey

Copyright © 1998 by Infinity Plus One, L.L.C. All rights reserved. No part
of this publication may be reproduced in whole or in part, or stored in an
information retrieval system, or transmitted in any form or by any means,
including electronic, mechanical, photocopying, recording, or otherwise,
without written permission from the publisher.

ISBN: 1-58260-006-6

Printed in the U.S.A.

10 9 8 7 6 5 4 3 2 1

Contents

●●

Chapter 1	The Story	7
Chapter 2	Dawson Leery	10
Chapter 3	Joey Potter	17
Chapter 4	Jennifer Lindley	23
Chapter 5	Pacey Witter	28
Chapter 6	James Van Der Beek	33
Chapter 7	Katie Holmes	51
Chapter 8	Michelle Williams	65
Chapter 9	Joshua Jackson	77
Chapter 10	Kevin Williamson	96
Chapter 11	The First Season	100
Chapter 12	What's the Buzz?	107
Chapter 13	Test Your Knowledge	113
Chapter 14	Rockin' on the Creek	119
Chapter 15	Hot Sites for Cool Info	122

1

The Story

It's the hottest new show on television with the coolest new stars. It's the show everybody's talking about—and the characters we're all dying to meet. But how much do you really know about the cast and characters of *Dawson's Creek*? What's the low-down on Dawson, Joey, Jen, and Pacey? What are the actors who play them really like? Who came up with the idea for *Dawson's Creek*? What's it like being on location in Wilmington, North Carolina? You'll be surprised by how much you didn't know—and by how much you will soon!

How would you like to live in a house that

backed up to a creek? Would you like to be able to take a boat to go visit your friends? Dawson and Joey do that every day on Dawson's Creek. *Dawson's Creek* is set in the fictional town of Capeside, Massachusetts, which is somewhere outside of Boston and just a ferry ride away from Rhode Island. Capeside is a small quaint town that thrives on summer tourism and quiets down during the off-seasons.

One of the creeks running through town runs right behind Dawson Leery's house. He and his best friend, Joey Potter (who's a girl, of course), have to row across the creek whenever they want to see each other. And when Dawson feels like visiting Jen, he doesn't have to go very far either—just next door. Jen Lindley, who recently moved to Capeside from New York City, lives with her grandparents right next door to Dawson. Pacey Witter, Dawson's best (male) friend, lives just a little further away in town.

Dawson's Creek is their story—the story of four fifteen-year-old friends, Dawson, Joey, Jen, and Pacey—and the troubles they run into as they try to grow up. During the first season, we learned that Dawson and Joey have been best friends for years, but now hormones threaten to change their relationship. Jen led a wild and fast-paced life in New York City and was sent to Capeside by her parents so she could try to settle down (and not to help her grandmother take care of her ill grandfather, as she originally told Dawson and the others). Pacey, even though he has a history of striking out with girls his age, manages to score with one of his teachers, and looks like he may have some potential with teenage girls, too. They each have their own unique lives, but they share the same basic problems—how to deal with a first love, first kiss, and first heartbreak. Those are the problems the show really focuses on—and the ones that keep us glued to the TV week after week!

2

Dawson Leery

Dawson Leery, the title character of the show, is something of a film buff. Well, actually, he's more of a film nut. Crazy about director Steven Spielberg (it's all he thinks about, 24/7), Dawson has created an homage to Spielberg on his bedroom wall. It's made up of all kinds of Spielberg movie posters and memorabilia. He even has an E.T. doll on his bed (and when Dawson has to explain himself to Jen's boyfriend from New York, we find out that it's not just any doll, it's a collector's item). Dawson is such a film fanatic that he plans on becoming a filmmaker when he grows up. He's off to a good start, too. He has already written, directed, and produced his own movie, *Sea Serpent from the Deep,* using Jen, Joey, and Pacey to play the characters. And not only did he write it, produce it, and film it, Dawson also sent it off to a Boston film contest to compete against hundreds of other films.

Dawson's obsession leads him to try to get into the school's film class, even though he's just a sophomore and the course is reserved for juniors and seniors. Although the teacher completely rejects his application, Dawson refuses to give up. He finally gets transferred to the film class during his study hall period. (His excuse is that the library study hall is too crowded.) He also has to promise his teacher that he won't participate in the class, and that he will be merely an observer and nothing more. Well, Dawson may have promised to be quiet, but he should have known he couldn't pull it off. He very quickly makes a nuisance of himself by pestering the teacher with questions. Then, during the filming of the class's movie, *Helmets of Glory,* he finds himself on the wrong side of the producer, Nellie Olsen. Nellie has taken a dislike to him because she doesn't feel he's paid his dues to earn a place in the film class. But Dawson saves the day when he solves the problem of how to film while running backwards—instead of running, he has the cameraman sit in a wheelchair that gets pulled backwards. The shot comes out perfectly, and Dawson, thanks to his extensive film knowledge, is the hero.

There's more to Dawson's life than just films, though. Beyond his interest in movies, his life has been defined by his friendship with Joey. They're such good friends that Dawson leaves a ladder perched against his windowsill so Joey can have easy access to his room. There's nothing romantic going on between them, though—at least not to Dawson's knowledge. He seems incapable of seeing Joey as anything more than his best friend. There are times when he even seems incapable of seeing her as a girl. Dawson confides everything in Joey, including his troubles with girls, and then waits for her to give him the advice that will make it all better. He often treats Joey as if she is the fourth member of his family, the sister he never had.

Dawson's an only child and gets along very well with both his parents, although his family life has recently been turned upside down.

During a hurricane, and after being confronted by both Joey and Dawson, Dawson's mother confesses to him and his father that she's been having an affair. Dawson feels totally shocked; his whole world has been rocked. What makes it so hard to believe is that his parents have always been so affectionate with each other. Dawson has always had to knock before he goes into any room in the house, because he doesn't want to "accidentally" interrupt them, and he has often lamented that his parents' sex life is better than his (nonexistent) own.

When confronted with the knowledge of his mother's affair, Dawson does just what he always does when there's something wrong. He runs to Joey. And when Joey lets Dawson know that she already knew about the affair (she just can't lie to him!), Dawson again characteristically reacts a little too dramatically. Joey weathers the hurricane and Dawson's temper out together, and sure enough, he comes back to her.

It's not the first time Dawson has overreacted, and it probably won't be the last, especially with someone like Jen Lindley in his life. Dawson, romantic and dramatic to his very core, falls head over heels in love with the mysterious girl from New York. Playing the role of the honorable gentleman from his black-and-white movies, Dawson moves slowly with Jen, waiting for quite some time before giving her so much as a kiss. Joey, always the realistic one, reminds Dawson that there's a fine line between being a gentleman and being stupid. Dawson's thoughtfulness is endearing, though, and his talk with his dad about what makes a perfect kiss is nothing less than adorable. It's with Jen that all of Dawson's cutest traits come out—his sweetness, his romantic nature, his dedication, but most of all, the fact that he is totally and completely oblivious to the real world. After all, he's so wrapped up in Jen that he can't see that his best friend is madly in love with him. And he gives his imagination free reign to decide what his future with Jen will be like. In this, as in many things, Dawson chooses a romanticized version of life over the reality of it all.

Dawson's biggest problem with reality comes whenever he tries to script it and direct it just like he would a movie. He routinely uses movie vocabulary when he's explaining his actions. For instance, he tells Pacey, "It's time for a rewrite," and then crosses the room dramatically to try and cut in on Jen and Cliff (the star athlete) dancing. He's cast himself as one of the nice guys, and Jen as the mysterious-but-innocent girl that the hero is going to sweep off her feet. The fact that Jen's his first girlfriend makes her extremely important to him. Dawson takes forever to kiss her because he wants it to be perfect, but all he ends up doing is scaring her. Jen's afraid that he's built up the kiss so much that he'll be disappointed when the real Jen and the real kiss don't measure up to the scripted ones. Their first kiss doesn't go as Dawson plans—they end up talking and dancing in the middle of the atmosphere he had designed—but instead they wind up being totally spontaneous and improvising. Who knows? Maybe it's a way to show Dawson that he needs to visit reality a little more.

Dawson sees his love for Jen as an extension of his love for Joey. In a particularly irritating speech he tells Joey that she has all of the same qualities Jen has (or rather that Jen has all of the same qualities Joey has) and that Jen could be Joey . . . but she's Jen. Huh?!

The most dysfunctional aspect of Dawson's relationship with Jen is the way he fights with her. Their first fight concerns the facts surrounding Jen's move to Capeside. When Dawson learns that Jen has quite a past (sexually, that is), and why her parents sent her to Capeside, he just can't deal with it. Afterwards, whenever he gets angry with her, Dawson tends to make some very thinly veiled reference to her sex life in New York. For someone who sees himself as such a nice guy, Dawson really does have to apologize a lot! Maybe if he just stops trying to prove himself to everyone, he'd be able to relax a little. And doesn't Dawson realize that girls *love* good guys? Stay sweet, Dawson—we love you just the way you are!

3

Joey Potter

It would be hard to have a life with more obstacles and bad luck than Joey Potter has faced. What's gone wrong? Here's a quick run-down: her mother's dead from breast cancer, her father's in jail for drug trafficking (after running around and cheating on her mother before she died!), and her unmarried sister just had a baby. Joey lives with her sister, Bessie, Bessie's black boyfriend, Bodie, and their new baby. She also lives in a small house on "the wrong side of the creek." Unfortunately for Joey, in a little town like Capeside, living arrangements like that are an automatic bad rap, no matter how good a kid you are. On top of all that, Joey is finding that the only stable thing in her life—her relationship with Dawson—is turning upside down. Even though she tells Dawson that she's afraid "hormones" will cause a falling out in their relationship, she still finds herself falling in love with him more and more each day. And no matter how obvious Joey thinks she is about it, Dawson remains blissfully unaware of her feelings for him. Even when Joey breaks down crying in the library and says there's something she needs to tell him, Dawson remains utterly clueless. However, her crush has not escaped the notice of the more astute Pacey and Jen. But like Joey, they don't have any idea what to do about it but sit and wait for Dawson to notice. Joey contents herself with being what she's always been—Dawson's best friend and confidante and the fourth member of the Leery household.

And speaking of the Leery household, Joey is the first one to find out about Mrs. Leery's affair. Wise beyond her years, she confronts Mrs. Leery with an eloquent and forceful speech. We know that Joey's father, in addition to everything else he did, also cheated on her mother.

Joey tells Mrs. Leery just how much that kind of unfaithfulness can hurt a family. Joey's speech is one of the main reasons that Mrs. Leery decides to end her affair and confess to her husband and Dawson.

Speeches like the one she gave to Dawson's mom are what Joey does best. They also serve as her shield against the world. Most of the time Joey adds in a bit more sarcasm than she uses with Dawson's mom. After being dealt such a rough hand in life, Joey has a lot of experience sticking up for herself. Though her first resort is always verbal, she's not afraid to get physical. In "The Breakfast Club" episode, Joey lands in Saturday detention for flooring the dumb jock who was giving her a hard time. But if there's anyone she gives a hard time to, it's Dawson. Joey seems to see it as her duty as Dawson's best friend to balance out his romantic and dramatically colored view of the world with her own unique brand of realism, cynicism, and snappy retorts. The two of them are so close that when she comes over she goes, quite literally, directly to his room. For years she has entered the Leery house through Dawson's bedroom window, thanks to the ladder he keeps leaned up against the sill. It doesn't matter whether or not Dawson's home when Joey arrives, or even if he's sleeping. She's always welcome there, and Dawson often comes home to find her waiting for him in his room. Sometimes, like the time he got back from a night with the boys in Providence, Dawson falls asleep with Joey sitting up in his bed, or they even fall asleep together, just as they've done since they were little kids. However, nothing sexual goes on between them (although Joey has pointed out that it may be a little awkward and inappropriate for them to continue this sleepover-friends routine). And Joey continues to reassure Dawson that she's known him too long to have a "thang" (thing) for him.

Joey's chosen enemy is Jen Lindley, Dawson's love interest. Even though Jen has told Joey repeatedly that she wants to make it impossible for Joey not to like her, Joey somehow surmounts every obstacle of kindness Jen throws in her way and still manages to be sarcastic and spiteful around her. Joey enjoys skewering Jen in passing with remarks like, "I love your hair color—what number is it?" Joey knows she shouldn't hate Jen, but she doesn't seem to be able to help it. It doesn't help much that Jen and Dawson are always hanging around together, or that Dawson talks about nothing but Jen. Jen-this, Jen-that, I like Jen so much, Jen's so great, isn't she Joey? It's hard not to hate someone when the person you're in love with is in love with that someone. Still, Joey admits to Jen that she wishes Jen could just be "a wench" so that at least there'd be more of a reason to hate her. Unfortunately for Joey, Jen's just not the wench type.

After school, Joey works at the S.S. Icehouse, an outdoor restaurant run by Bessie and Bodie. It's a tourist-y kind of place, and like the town of Capeside, it flourishes in the summer and is   pretty empty come wintertime. It's a lot of work, and with the arrival of Bessie's and Bodie's baby, the stress really seems to be wearing on Joey. Between Joey's work at the restaurant, her schoolwork, her problems with Jen and Dawson, and the baby's sleepless nights, Joey's running low on steam. One of the few bright spots has been her fling with Anderson, a rich kid who was staying on his yacht in Capeside. Joey fabricated way too many stories about herself to ever allow for a long-term relationship with Anderson, but it made her feel good to be wanted—even if it was just for a short time.

Joey's friends take care of her, though. Dawson lets her crash at his house, and Pacey watches over her when she gets too tired and upset (and accidentally drunk) to watch out for herself. Pacey, in fact, makes the ultimate sacrifice—he recites the story of *The English Patient,* a movie that, in his opinion, "blows," to calm the baby down when he starts crying. The problem is that when Joey gets tired, she loses control over her tightly guarded self. Dawson and Pacey bring her back to her house to put her to sleep, and in her stupor she sits up and gives Dawson a kiss. Poor, oblivious Dawson still doesn't get it. Rowing back to his house with Pacey, he dismisses the kiss, saying that Joey probably just mistook him for Brad Pitt or something. Pacey knows that's not what happened, but Dawson's skull is so thick he doesn't understand what Pacey is saying to him. From her sleepy state, Joey gave herself a golden opportunity to make Dawson understand, but he still didn't get it. It'll be interesting to see if he ever does. As Joey told Jen, she's willing to wait for just the right guy—and it sounds as if Dawson is the perfect guy for her.

4

Jennifer Lindley

While life hasn't been easy for Jen, she sure hasn't had it as bad as Joey. She admits that her life in New York City wasn't all that innocent. In fact, she was shipped off to her grandparents' house because her parents caught her having sex on their bed with her boyfriend. As far as the town is concerned, however, she was sent to Capeside to help take care of her ailing grandfather. Jen and her grandmother make a fiery combination. Jen is an atheist (meaning she doesn't believe in God), while her grandmother is devoutly religious. Her grandmother is also extremely opinionated. She has very definite opinions on the people in the town, and she's not too shy to share them with her granddaughter and anyone else who will listen.

Jen's having a lot of trouble adjusting to life in Capeside. Or, more accurately, Capeside is having a lot of trouble adjusting to life with Jen. The adults in town, and even some of the kids, seem to resent Jen for having lived in the big, fast-paced city all of her life. Some of her teachers even take pains to tell her that while she may have gotten away with "that kind of behavior" in the big, immoral city, she won't get away with it in Capeside. Poor Jen lands in Saturday detention for disagreeing with one of these close-minded moralizers on the subject of assisted suicide. When the teacher announces to the class what their opinion on the issue will be, Jen disagrees with him. It turns out that in New York students are allowed to have discussions with their teachers, but in Capeside, students are expected to sit down, be quiet, and agree with the all-knowing teacher. It's not hard to understand why Jen doesn't go along with that kind of thinking.

While she may be having some trouble with the teachers, Jen's doing pretty well with the boys. As soon as she moves in, Dawson falls head over heels in love with her and half the boys in town are positively drooling over her. She chooses Dawson, but is guilty of having extremely mixed feelings about other boys and her relationship with Dawson. Jen wants to take things slowly because she's unsure, but Dawson is certain that it would be great to move things along quickly. (One of her best speeches to Dawson involves the positive side of taking their relationship slowly: "Look at it this way, Dawson. Repressing desire can only make it more powerful. So I figure the next time I see you, we are in for one Titanic kiss.") Jen even finds herself attracted to Pacey— perhaps more than she is attracted to Dawson. Although Jen realizes that the real reason she becomes involved with Dawson is that he's a nice guy— the kind of guy a girl should be going out with— she also knows that it's not a good sign that she doesn't exactly have the hots for Dawson. Sure, he's cute...but Pacey might be cuter.

Poor Dawson. He knows he should be happy that he has the girl. He also knows that it's better to be liked because of his personality than because of his appearances...but it sure would be great to have Jen want him because of his body, too! What's hardest to believe is that Jen doesn't find Dawson drop-dead gorgeous. The rest of the teenage girls in the free world are completely in lust with him, and Jen is able to keep him at arms' length. So the question is, what kind of boys was she seeing in New York?

It doesn't take long to get the answer to that question. Much to Joey's delight, Dawson's dismay, and the utter confusion of Jen, Jen's ex-boyfriend Billy makes a surprise appearance in Capeside. Billy's visit makes Jen realize what she wants from her life in Capeside and from her relationship with Dawson. She tells Dawson that she doesn't want to be using him as an escape from life's realities. Jen's afraid that she always runs into relationships to avoid being on her own or to avoid having to deal with her problems—like adjusting to life in Capeside. So Jen decides that she doesn't want to be going out with anyone—not even Dawson—until she's had some time on her own to learn more about herself and what kind of person she really is. Coming from someone who hasn't spent a Friday night at home alone since she was thirteen, that's a big decision. Especially because there is a seemingly endless supply of guys in Capeside who would be thrilled to go out with her. Jen's decided, though, that her New York City life was just too fast. She did too much too soon and now she's being given a chance to slow down a bit.

Unfortunately for Jen, boys aren't the only problem in her life. Jen's biggest problem is Joey. It must be frustrating to try so hard to be nice to someone and only get back nasty remarks. Jen's pretty honest with Joey, though—she tells her right from the beginning that her goal is to make it impossible for Joey not to like her. And she does a pretty good job at it. Joey can only come up with one real reason to hate Jen: because Dawson loves her. Jen doesn't do a single thing that Joey can hate her for beyond that, and Joey knows it's unreasonable to expect Jen to have control over Dawson's emotions. So Joey hates Jen because Dawson's in love with her, but Jen knows the truth of it. The two girls agree that Dawson's only in love with one of them—and they're both sure it's the other person that he loves. Jen is most likely the one who's right, though—she knows that she is probably just a temporary infatuation, and that one day Dawson will realize that Joey is his one and only.

5

Pacey Witter

It's the character of Pacey Witter who got *Dawson's Creek* off to a wild start, giving the show its raciest action and dialogue. Telling her that he's "the best sex you'll never have," the boy who never gets the girls all of a sudden finds himself with quite a woman—his English teacher, Tamara Jacobs, who is about 20 years older than he is. Thanks to the characters of Pacey and Tamara, *Dawson's Creek* premiered to magazine and newspaper articles not concerned with the show itself, but with the morality of this relationship. What makes their relationship so interesting is that it's not Tamara who does the seducing—it's Pacey. Each time Tamara tries to break off their relationship Pacey goes after her again, looking so sweet and talking so persuasively that Tamara finally gives in. In school the day after their first kiss, Tamara tries to tell Pacey that nothing happened the night before and that nothing would ever happen again. Pacey, with characteristic bluntness, tells her that something most definitely *did* happen!

One reason why his relationship with Tamara is so important to him is that Pacey feels very disconnected from his family. His father and brother hold fairly important positions in the town—his father's the sheriff and his brother's a deputy. But Pacey has never gone in for the whole law-enforcement thing, so he's never really felt that comfortable with his dad and brother. He feels a lot more comfortable with his older sisters and his mother. But since his three sisters are away at college, he's left with only his mother to talk to. Pacey's family makes a point of telling him that he's a screw-up and will never succeed. Because of their lack of support, Pacey feels like it doesn't matter what he does.

And it's not as if Pacey gets any support from his classmates, either. Remember Nellie Olsen's speech to him in the video store? "Do I need to remind you of who you are?" she says to Pacey. "Nobody. That's the point. You're not here. You don't even exist." Pacey has decided that as long as he's never going to succeed at anything, he may as well do whatever he wants.

Because he doesn't have his family's support, Pacey looks outside to find people who appreciate him. He is Dawson's best (male) friend and the third member of the longstanding Dawson-Joey-Pacey gang. He's an extremely loyal friend—mostly because their friendship is so important to him. When Joey's about to crash because of the baby, school, and work, it's Pacey who really comes through for her. He kidnaps her from the S.S. Icehouse and drags her to a beach party. He says he's tired of her never going out and doing anything for herself. Unfortunately, Joey gets a little drunk at the beach party and finds herself in a very vulnerable position with a not-very-nice guy. Pacey tries to intervene before she gets smashed but Joey brushes him off. Once she's in real danger, though, he stops letting her send him away. He separates Joey from the mean guy and ends up knocking him out. Even though a delirious Joey gives Dawson all of the credit, Pacey doesn't complain. He and Dawson both know that the credit is Pacey's, and that's enough for them.

Interestingly enough, it's Pacey who often ends up as the voice of reason for the gang. While Dawson assures himself that Joey just mistook him for Brad Pitt when she kissed him, Pacey laughs at the dream world his friend is living in. It hasn't escaped Pacey's notice that Joey's madly in love with Dawson—or that Dawson, even if he doesn't know it, is madly in love with Joey. One of his cutest lines comes while Jen's ex-boyfriend Billy is creating chaos in town. When Joey comes by Screenplay Video, the video store both Pacey and Dawson work at, Pacey takes the opportunity to grill her about Dawson, Jen, and Billy. He finally regards her with a satisfied look in his eyes and says, "You're really enjoying having Jen's ex in town, aren't you?" Once again, Pacey cuts to the quick of the situation and (very correctly) figures out what's going on.

Pacey may also be the most intelligent and mature member of the Dawson's Creek gang. That's one reason why an older woman would be interested in him, and one reason why Dawson and Joey want to hang around with Pacey—he's definitely older and wiser than his years.

6

James Van Der Beek

Growing Up

Like the kids in Capeside, James grew up in a small NewEngland town. He also vacationed in Cape Cod (where the show is set) every summer with his family. (And he may very well have had a few good summer romance stories that could be worked into the Dawson's Creek plot lines!) James describes his family as extremely supportive. His entire family, and especially his mother, made a lot of sacrifices to support his acting career—but we'll get into all that a little bit later in this chapter. James was born on March 8, 1977, which makes him 21 at the end of the show's pilot season, and the oldest of the cast members.

James is the oldest of three kids and grew up in the small Connecticut town of Cheshire. His brother, Jared, is three years younger than James, and his sister, Juliana, is five years younger. (Can you imagine the attention she must get in her high school with a brother like James?) His dad, Jim, is an executive at a cellular phone company, and once pitched for the Los Angeles Dodgers. His mom, Melinda, used to be a Broadway dancer and now owns a gymnastics studio in town. James is a terrific gymnast, but then again, he's good at almost all sports. When he was younger, James used to be a football player. In fact, it was a minor injury from playing football that changed the course of James's life.

Sidelined for a Season

It may not be nice to be glad someone got hurt, but fans of *Dawson's Creek* will agree—it's a good thing an injury sidelined James from football. If it weren't for a minor concussion James got at the age of 13, he might never have begun acting—and he never would have become Dawson.

Here's the story: James used to be a football

player (he still loves playing sports). In eighth grade in his school gym class, he was playing football and went out for a pass. He fell and got a mild concussion. The doctors told him he couldn't play football that year. Since he was sidelined, James decided to do something with his newfound free time. He tried out for a local children's theatre production of *Grease*. He did well for his first audition—well enough to land the lead role of Danny Zuko (played by John Travolta in the movie version). "They dyed my hair black, and I was still a boy soprano," he said. He may have been a soprano, but he nevertheless managed to snag his first girlfriend. As for the acting, "I loved it," James says. "I mean just absolutely loved it." The acting bug had bitten: James was hooked. He kept trying out for community and school plays and kept getting great roles. "And then I really started developing an intense interest in performing and it was just this whole new world I was incredibly excited by," he adds. It was just a matter of what to do next. So he started making...

The Trips to New York City (or, What a Nice Mom!)

By the time James was 16 years old, he was

still going strong in community and school productions and his mom decided to make him an offer. The summer after he turned 16, she told James she would take him into New York City so he could try pursuing a professional career. Says James, "My mother kind of noticed my interest in [acting] and realized, wow, he's really into this, and said, 'If you want to try this, I will give you the opportunity this summer to go in and have a shot at it.' I think she kind of secretly hoped that maybe I would go in and realize it's a very tough business and it's very difficult and not want to do it." So his mom took the train into the Big Apple with him to try to get him started. Their first trip to the city was relatively successful—James landed an agent and a personal manager. Their next trips didn't go as well. James spent an entire year unsuccessfully auditioning for commercials. He still says that commercials are the one kind of job that he just can't seem to get. "Cereal. Candy. Everything. I still can't get booked."

James remembers the trips into New York that summer. "We'd make our sandwiches before we'd go and get on the Metro North train and go and then walk instead of taking cabs.

We'd be running around in the hot summer, dropping off head shots at agents' offices. They'd open the door a crack and we'd feel the air conditioning. And they'd just grab the head shot, thank you, and shut the door."

He's thankful that his mom wasn't one of the "stage mothers" that many other young actors have. Because she had been a professional dancer, she knew "kind of how it works and how not to really get screwed and kind of how to start," James explains. She was never one of those mothers James saw at his auditions, the ones combing their sons hair, telling them " 'don't say it like that, say it like that.' " James says he's "so glad my mother didn't start me off that way."

He says that his mother jokes about his interest in theatre sometimes. "She had two boys and so my dad is, like, all right, and then she had a little girl. When my sister was six and my mom brought her to a dance recital and asked my sister, 'Isn't this exciting?' My sister's, like, 'No.' 'You don't like this?' And my sister's, like, 'Not really. I don't think I want to do this next year.' So my mom kind of resigned herself. And then all of a sudden I was 15 years old and I was doing a show and I needed to tap dance. My mother bought me tap shoes and she's going, 'I never thought I'd be buying tap shoes for any of my kids, least of all my first-born son.' So it was really kind of funny the way it worked out."

James' big break came when he auditioned for the off-Broadway play, *Finding the Sun*, which was written and directed by three-time Pulitzer Prize winning playwright Edward Albee. He made the cut and was cast in the role of Fergus. And so began the months of long rehearsals, and then the three-month limited run of the show. Every rehearsal required a three-hour trip into the city, and when rehearsal was over, the three-hour return trip was waiting. His mother accompanied him each time, and waited for him during every rehearsal.

Sounds like a full schedule, right? Well that's not all James was doing. He was finishing his senior year in high school, which meant that he was going to school during the day, rehearsing in the evenings, and doing his schoolwork in any free time he could find. With all of this going on, he still managed to finish second in his high school class and be a member of the National Honor Society. Talk about talent!

James credits this play as a "defining experience" in his development as an actor.

After his success with *Finding the Sun*, James went on to star in the Goodspeed Opera House's production of *Shenandoah*, and in 1997 he appeared in another off-Broadway play, *My Marriage To Ernest Borgnine*.

Moving on Up

James got another big break in 1995, during his senior year of high school, when he was cast in the feature film *Angus*. He played Rick Sanford, an arrogant jock. James was very excited about the movie. "Everybody was telling me, 'Oh, wow, this is going to be huge for you, you're going to be a big star.' OK, cool, and I waited. Nothing happened. Basically the movie didn't do very well; it didn't propel me to where they said it would. So now I take all this type of thing with a grain of salt."

It may not have propelled him, but it didn't stop him. After *Angus*, James landed roles in Miramax's *I Love You...I Love You Not*, starring Claire Danes. His next movie was *Harvest*, starring *Private Parts*' Mary McCormack, an independent film about a group of farmers who come into hard times and decide to grow marijuana.

He didn't just find work in movies, though. James also appeared on television in roles such as Paul on Nickelodeon's *Clarissa Explains It All,* and in after-school specials such as ABC's *The Red Booth.* And you soap-opera fans out there may remember him as the adorable young Stephen on *As the World Turns.*

Once he started college at Drew University in Madison, New Jersey, James had a rough time finding employment. His auditions weren't going well and James says, "I just did terrible." He finally gave up and left it all. "What I did was I took six weeks off," James says. "I just packed up and took six weeks off from being an actor and traveled around Europe and came back and said, yeah, this is exactly what I want to do."

Landing Dawson

James's audition for *Dawson's Creek* was a pain. He had to miss school to go into New York City (again!) for the audition. After his audition James was invited to fly out to Los Angeles for a screen test. "I'm twenty years old," he said, questioning their decision. Why would they want him to play a fifteen-year-old? After reading the script, though, he felt differently. "I thought, Oooh, I really want to do this. I hope I didn't just talk myself out of the job." He shouldn't have been nervous about talking himself out of the job—he should have been nervous about being too nervous! Kevin Williamson, the creator of the show, explains that he had to calm James down. "He was really nervous, and it showed. Then he came back into the room and stunned us. We knew he was Dawson. He's very bright, but he's also very vulnerable. I like that, because that keeps him fifteen years old," Kevin says.

James landed the role within three days; he was all of the producers' first choice almost immediately after his audition. Executive producers Kevin Williamson and Paul Stupin may have favored him for the role of Dawson, but they were a little worried about his hair. Says James, "Someone made the comment about my hair being too long, so Paul drove me around frantically to get me a haircut." Hair freshly cut, James was a shoe-in for the role. But in order to film the series, James had to take time off from college. An excellent student, James had received an academic scholarship from the school, was named to the dean's list, and had just been awarded the Drew University Presidential Scholarship. Although currently on leave from

41

college, James is pursuing a major in English and a minor in sociology. When asked what career he would choose if he hadn't landed the role of Dawson, James answered, "I'd probably be a teacher. Middle-school teacher. I had a real mentor from middle school, and it's such a miserable time for any kid." (Is there any middle-school girl who wouldn't love to have James as her English teacher?!) But now that he's got the role of Dawson, what does he think of it all?

James On Dawson

"I can definitely relate" to Dawson, says James. "He's a lot like I was at fifteen—innocent, idealistic, impassioned, and often clueless." The similarities continue. "Dawson and I were both very impassioned at an early age. Dawson is a burgeoning film maker, whose overactive imagination and idealism sometimes make him oblivious. He's prone to rejecting reality for a more romantic scenario. He's a bit of an innocent and is frequently off in his own little world, all of which I can definitely relate to." And, jokes James, "We also look alike."

"He's the dork in all of us, I think," James says of Dawson. "Dawson does all the things you want to do but you're afraid to do because of what will happen. Dawson does that, and then it happens anyway, and then you watch." He adds, "The mistakes Dawson makes stem from ignorance. The whole boy-girl thing...he's finding his way."

What does James think about the eloquent dialogue used by the show's main characters? Some critics of the show think that it makes the characters less real when they speak so articulately. James admits that "Dawson can process his emotions and verbalize them in a way that not everybody can, but anybody who's ever gone through adolescence can relate to him." And all teenagers shouldn't be grouped in one big articulate lump, James believes. "There are definitely kids who speak that way and who think that way," he states. "And while the dialogue isn't necessarily representative of the way every kid speaks, it's absolutely representative of how every kid feels, which I think is much more important."

So what's the show about, according to James? At first, he gives the standard TV studio response: "*Dawson's Creek* is an hour drama series of four teenagers in a suburb of Boston coming of age...dealing with teenage issues."

But what does that really mean? James boils it down for us—"So in other words sex, sex, [and] more sex." Does he find that all of this talk about sex is a bit much? Nope, says the actor, "It's honest and it's fairly responsible without being preachy."

Speaking of sexual references, James has a lot to say about the scripts and the controversy over the amount of sex in the show. First of all, he says, "It's been adults mainly who have the problem. No one under twenty has said, 'That's too much sex; that's not the way it really is.'" And, he says, there's really not that much serious sex. "There's one kiss, there's one almost-kiss. I think my response to that is always, you know, we're not giving these kids any ideas, we're not talking about things they aren't already thinking about. I think it's good that we talk about them and that we talk about them responsibly. I was baffled by the number of people who were upset."

James has nothing but praise for Kevin Williamson's scripts, especially his dialogues. "I think one of the great things is that the dialogue that we have is what kids are thinking about and coping with, but aren't necessarily talking about." He responds to criticism of the scripts by saying, "I think the intentions behind the words are absolutely real and absolutely honest, and I don't think they're exaggerating. I think kids are a lot smarter than the media gives them credit for. I think they really are a lot more aware than adults often give them credit for. I think it's really great that they are able to—on this show, that they're able to speak about—about such confusing things. I don't think we say anything in this show that 15-year-olds aren't thinking or feeling. I don't think there's been a thing said on the show that isn't a fairly universal theme."

Hanging Out In Wilmington

On location in Wilmington, North Carolina, James rooms with co-star Josh Jackson, who plays Pacey. "We got along very well . . . he had a dog and we were both looking for apartments and we found this really cool place that we split." He admits that the entire cast sees each other "probably more than is healthy." It's hard not to, though. "We're all isolated down there," he explains. "We're away from our homes, our families, our friends, the rest of the business."

He says that he and Josh are "the odd couple." Adds Josh, "People called us the Odd Couple, and I was definitely not Felix." James says that there really aren't any problems being roommates. "Nothing beyond the norm," he explains. "I shower first and I'm eating up the hot water, you know, all the normal stuff." They're certainly not big TV watchers, considering they've become television stars. "We watch football on the weekends, that's about it. That's the only thing we watch." In the little free time the actors have (they work up to 14 hours a day), James uses his time pretty simply. "Sleep," he says. "Sleep, read, you know, listen to music. I'm teaching myself how to play the guitar." (And, just in case you were wondering, James wears boxers, not briefs.)

The rest of the cast has plenty to say about the boy playing squeaky-clean Dawson. First of all, says Josh, James is just as sweet and earnest as Dawson. "He's the good-looking, polite, college-educated kid who says 'sir' and 'ma'am.'" Michelle Williams describes James as having "a Cary Grant quality." Kevin Williamson, the show's creator, thinks that "James is going to be a huge star. He's very serious and single-minded about acting. But what is nice about him and the other kids is that they're unaffected. They're not yet stars, so they're not concerned with the size of their trailer...yet!"

James has been away at college for several years (he left during his sophomore year, and he would have been a second semester junior at the time of the show's premiere) so he doesn't miss his family in the same way his other co-stars do. There are some people he misses, though. His best friend, Sarah, is still at Drew University. He denies any romantic involvement between the two, saying, "We're best friends, it's really cool." (Sort of like Dawson and Joey, huh?)

James feels that his biggest task is keeping up with the grueling pace of the show. "The greatest challenge is trying to come up and consistently do good work in such a short amount of time. The pace is really, very, very difficult. Here we get a script, we're shooting something, maybe if we're lucky we get a read-through. Actually, the sheer memorization part of it is hard, just to try to sit there and memorize eight pages of dialogue after you've been working 14 hours and you've got to get to bed if you want to get eight hours sleep, just 'cause you have to and you'll die if you don't."

Publicity Whirlwind

It's been a crazy ride promoting *Dawson's Creek*. Not to mention a lot of limo rides, too. James said it was "weird enough" riding around L.A. in a limo in January, but when he looked outside and saw himself on a billboard, he says, "I just started laughing because I didn't know how to deal with the hype. I kept asking myself, 'How did I get here?'" As for Los Angeles, James says "L.A. is such a surreal experience." He had a lot of cool experiences while promoting the show in L.A. "They took me around and showed me the whole Hollywood scene. I saw people wearing sunglasses at night! I always thought that was a joke, but they really do it!"

Working with Kevin Williamson has its perks, too. James was at a party at Kevin's house and he thought it was so cool because "Kevin to me was Kevin." He's been surprised by the amount of attention the show has received. At the same party, James says, "I was sitting there and Buffy the Vampire Slayer came up and said, 'Hey, I love your show.' That was really weird." Buffy's not the only one who's been giving Dawson's some positive praise. James heard "that Steven Spielberg saw it and loved it, had his secretary call Kevin and say that he liked it. That was another weird moment. Steven called!"

James first realized the extent of the Dawson's hype when he went to the network announcement. "I walked in, and there was this movie screen, and they started playing, you know, the *Dawson's Creek* trailer and I heard my voice and boom, there was the four of us, and we're all doing our thing and there's music in the background and it's really cool. I was like, wow, and I turned around and like every network exec, I think, was there." What was his reaction to the evening? "I ran back to my friend's apartment and called the other three, I was 'Oh, my God, you guys, you've got to listen to what people are saying about this.' And that was quite a trip."

His friends back at school aren't that fazed by James's rapid rise to fame. "Well, I got a whole core group of friends who are excited for me because I'm doing what I want to do. But you know they're really not any more impressed than they would be if I was promoted to assistant manager in McDonald's." (OK, that's just a little hard to believe!)

James admits that he's a little weirded out by

the people asking him for autographs. "I always feel so detached from the people who recognize me, because they know the Dawson persona. They don't know me at all." That's not to say he's upset by the attention: "I'd be lying if I said I didn't think it was pretty cool."

Planning for the Future

In a ideal world James would get to work with Steven Spielberg (another way he relates to Dawson). He'd also love to work with Stanley Kubrik, Milos Forman, and Martin Scorsese. In terms of actors, "There's a huge list there. There's so many actors whose work I respect and admire, who I'd just love to be able to work with."

For right now, though, James is happy to be working at what he enjoys. He's signed a deal to star in Paramount's new movie, *Varsity Blues,* scheduled for release in late 1998. He will co-star with Jon Voight and play a second-string high-school quarterback who ends up a hero. Hey, how about a movie about a high-school quarterback who becomes a TV star?

7

Katie Holmes

Growing Up

Growing up in Toledo, Ohio, Katie Holmes never thought she'd make it as an actress — certainly not when she was living in the Midwest and not some California beach town. Katie was born on December 18, 1978, which makes her 19 years old at the end of the show's pilot season. Her father is a lawyer, her mother is a homemaker, and Katie is the youngest of their five kids. She has three older sisters and one older brother, all of whom are athletes. She attended Notre Dame Academy, a private, all-girls school in Toledo.

Says Katie about her life growing up, "I'm a small-town girl just like Joey. I was a little bit of a tomboy and also the youngest in my family, so I thought I knew everything." Katie may have thought she knew everything, but there's no way she could have predicted how quickly she would rise to fame. In fact, Katie never really believed she could make it as an actress starting from Toledo. "I wanted to be an actress, but I'm from Ohio," she explains. "I told myself, get a grip." Little did she know how much—and how fast—her life was going to change.

Catching a Rising Star

Like James, Katie started out acting in her high school plays. When she was younger, Katie felt that "Hollywood and its numerous success stories seemed extremely far away and definitely from a world that I would never come into contact with." That all changed when she attended the IMTA (International Modeling and Talent Association) New York Convention on July 23, 1995. In a ballroom at the New York Hilton, where the event was held, Katie performed a monologue in front of about fifty other contestants, plus Al Onorato, David Guillod, and Bobby Moresco of Onorato/Guillod

Entertainment. These three men were conducting "Prepare to Compete," the seminar Katie was attending that evening. After she presented her piece, the three gave her suggestions on how to make it even better. She performed it for them again, and later wrote, "It was clear to me that something very special occurred in that ballroom that evening."

Six months later Katie found herself in Los Angeles, preparing her audition for Ang Lee's film *The Ice Storm*. She had signed with Onorato/Guillord Entertainment and the three men had become her business managers. She was in L.A. for the six-week pilot season, a time when the TV season's new shows are all holding auditions. Writes Katie of this exciting time, "Being in that untouchable world, experiencing the life of a beginning actress, was surreal. Suddenly this strange path of life seemed so normal. I love it."

Fast forward about four months to May 21, 1996. We see Katie sitting in a make-up chair in a New York City studio, getting ready to start filming on *The Ice Storm*. Her audition in L.A. had obviously gone very well. She was cast in the film and played the part of Libbets Casey, the rich girlfriend of Paul Hood (played by Tobey Maquire). *The Ice Storm* is a film about the sexual revolution of the 1970's. It recently won the screenplay award from the Cannes Film Festival and was very well received by critics, though it wasn't widely released. When describing her experience on the set, Katie says that Ang Lee, who also directed *Sense and Sensibility*, is wonderful. "When I first arrived on the set, [Ang Lee] took me into the trailer and explained the part and made sure I was comfortable with it. He blocks the scene, lets you try it out, gives you input. Very hands on." Katie describes the cast and crew of *The Ice Storm*, which starred Kevin Kline, Sigourney Weaver, Elijah Wood, and Joan Allen, as "extremely focused, conscientious people who are completely unconcerned with the Hollywood myth."

Katie's role in *The Ice Storm* found her playing one scene "messed up" at a party, and another with her head in Tobey Maguire's lap. How did she prepare for these scenes? Says Katie, "I didn't have any experience with drugs, but I'd seen people who were drunk and high, and they always acted really tired, so that's the way I went." And having her head in Tobey's lap?

Katie's glad her mom wasn't in the room. "It was kind of embarrassing...I had to be mature and not giggle." The scene may have been embarrassing, but she has nice things to say about co-star Maguire. "He's a very talented actor, he was very generous as an actor, and a great friend."

After *The Ice Storm,* Katie was on her way up. But how did she manage to land the role of Joey Potter on *Dawson's Creek?* It's actually quite an interesting story.

Getting Joey

Katie had fared well the year before in California, but when the 1997 pilot season came along she turned down the opportunity to go back out to auditions in L.A. Instead, Katie stayed home in Toledo and performed in her high school's production of *Damn Yankees.* Actually, the play was the joint effort of two schools—Katie's all-girl Notre Dame Academy, and the all-boy St. John's Jesuit. Instead of sending Katie to auditions, Onorato/Guillod Entertainment sent a video of her around to various studios. The producers of *Dawson's Creek* liked it so much that they invited her to callbacks. Unfortunately, the callbacks were scheduled for the same time as the opening night performance of *Damn Yankees*. Katie, in the leading role of Lola, decided to stick with the play and her friends. Luckily, the producers were able to schedule another date for her callbacks and she got the part. Isn't it nice when doing the right thing and success go hand-in-hand?

Katie on Joey

"Like Joey, I made a lot of mistakes, but fortunately I haven't had the tragedy that she's experienced in her life," Katie says. It's hard to believe that someone who has been so successful at such a young age could have made as many mistakes as Katie alludes to. She says that she definitely relates to Joey, though. "Only a few girls get to be prom queens and get all the guys. Those girls are like Jen. Joey isn't the girl who gets all the guys. I wasn't like that, either, so I can relate." (Again, it seems hard to believe, but we'll take Katie's word for it!)

How does Katie describe her character? "Joey is a 15-year-old girl that uses a tough attitude as a guard because she's been through so much. She's been hurt so many times that she doesn't want to be vulnerable and put herself out there for everyone. She has to be tough. She lost her mom and her dad's in prison. She doesn't have the best reputation in town because her sister, Bessie, is pregnant by Bodie, her black boyfriend, and they all live together. Her relationship with Dawson has been the only stable thing in her life and now it's beginning to change." Adds Katie, "She's a nice person."

How does Katie feel about Joey's razor-sharp sarcasm? "Joey has to come back with her wit. It's the only way she knows how to deal with her pathetic existence." Also, says Katie, "Joey's full of emotions. I'm like her in that we both say what we feel, but Joey goes a little further. I wouldn't say a lot of the things she says." What do Katie's parents think of her character? "They just kind of laugh," she says.

And what about Joey's unrequited love for Dawson? Katie says she hasn't actually experienced that kind of love. However, she explains, "Everybody goes through that stage of having a crush on somebody without realizing it, or realizing it and not feeling the same way." She uses this to explain the way Joey and Dawson feel about each other. "You just combine all that, and you get somewhere in the middle of Joey and Dawson's relationship." What's great about playing Joey, who is younger than Katie? "It's nice to be older because you can look at the big picture, you can remember how you felt...I relate to it so much—I was just there," Katie confesses.

Life On Location

Being on location in Wilmington, North Carolina, is Katie's first time on her own. Katie graduated from high school in 1997, and was scheduled to go to Columbia University that fall. *Dawson's Creek* changed her plans, though, and now she's deferred her admission for a year in order to film Dawson's and to work on other projects (which we'll find out about in the next section of this chapter). She describes the change as "a dream. Going from a high school musical to go to this pilot. Getting to meet all these people...forming all these friendships, and all this buzz...it's crazy." And, unlike some of the other cast members, Katie definitely plans on watching the shows. "The others will probably say, 'Oh no, I won't watch,' but I'll admit that I'll be watching it, thinking, 'Oh, my God! I thought they were going to use a different take.'"

Katie lives near the other actors in downtown Wilmington, but she chose to have her own place on location. "I'm not the easiest person to live with," she confesses. "I'm kind of a slob. So for me to consider a roommate, it would have to be one of my sisters or something." Since her sisters aren't there, the choice seemed easy. She does hang out with Michelle and the rest of the cast, though. She and Michelle have gone to the beach together a couple of times, and at last check-in were trying to get a trip into Charleston or Myrtle Beach (both cities are nearby in South Carolina) planned so they could go shopping. The two Dawson's girls also like watching movies together (Katie lives above a video store). Two of their favorites are *Sixteen Candles* and *Pretty in Pink*.

Katie says that the four main cast members are "kind of forced to" hang out together in Wilmington, because the rest of the cast and crew are much older than they are. Katie gets along well with everyone in the cast, but jokingly complains that James and Josh often try to provoke her. "They always say things to get a rise out of me. Very outlandish things. And they succeed," she admits. Are you wondering what kinds of things these two innocent looking boys could be doing to get a rise out of even-tempered Katie? She's willing to tell us—"You know, they moon me." (And that makes her mad?)

But in spite of all the moonings, she's learning a lot from her fellow actors. "All of them are very worldly, so at first I was intimidated. But they are teaching me." They're also tattling on her—James Van Der Beek told one interviewer that even though Joey rows back and forth across the creek, Katie herself is no rower. "It's rigged," she admits. "They put a rope under the boat and pull it."

Luckily, the off-screen dynamics are a lot different from the on-screen ones. For one, says Katie, "I like Michelle, and I hope she likes me." When they all have time off (which isn't very often) Katie says they "usually go to a movie, or go out to dinner, and hang out at the boys' apartment." Doesn't sound like too bad a life! There is a downside, though. She says her biggest challenge is "just being on my own." Since she rooms by herself she often comes home to an empty apartment at night, which is quite a change for her. "I come from a large family and most of my siblings are still in Toledo." So how else does Katie spend her free time? Talking on the phone with her family, of course.

Busy as a Bee

It looks like Katie will be spending a lot

more time away from home in the next few years. Says co-star Josh, "Katie's doing, like, 35 movies." Well, not quite 35—it's more like three. But that's still quite a lot to be doing in one year, especially when you're already starring in a TV series—and especially when you just broke onto the national scene at the beginning of the year. Katie's so busy that she couldn't join the rest of the cast in New Orleans for the premiere of *Dawson's Creek* in January. She had to be in Vancouver for the filming of one of her new projects.

Katie has been cast in *Dawson's Creek* creator Kevin Williamson's new movie, *Killing Mrs. Tingle*. The film is about a group of high school students who plot to kill their most hated teacher, Mrs. Tingle. Katie's going to play the ringleader of the group, and Helen Mirren (star of *Prime Suspects*) will play Mrs. Tingle. The movie is scheduled to be released sometime in late 1998.

Another of Katie's projects is the horror/ thriller, *Disturbing Behavior,* directed by David Nutter and starring David Benton, Jimmy Marsden, Steve Clark, and Nick Stahl. It's also scheduled to be released sometime in 1998.

Katie's last project is the "gritty comedy" *Go*, directed by *Swingers* director Doug Liman, and written by John August. *Go* is the story of a check-out girl, a British drug pusher, and two aspiring actors whose paths cross in L.A. and then later in Las Vegas. Katie and Christina Ricci (from *The Addams Family*) will co-star. Filmed in the spring of 1998, it should be released in late 1998 or early 1999.

So for all of those Katie Holmes' fans out there (and judging by the number of internet sites dedicated to her, there are certainly a lot of you!), you'll have plenty of opportunities to see her in action. And don't worry about Katie—or any of the *Dawson's Creek* stars—leaving the show anytime soon to work exclusively in films. Each of the stars has committed to a five-year contract to do the show. That means lots of great episodes and plot twists and turns to come. (Of course, it also means that Kevin Williamson can torture the audience for years before Dawson and Joey commit to each other!)

And Katie doesn't have any plans to stop acting any time soon. She'd love to be in an Oliver Stone movie or a period piece like *Sense and Sensibility*. How does Katie see herself in ten years? "Married, with 1.5 children," she confides. "I hope I'm at a nice place in my career." Katie will be looking "to do things that are interesting and help me grow as an actor...do things that make me happy; projects that make me happy." She's not just thinking about her career, though. She also says that she hopes she's "in college or have already gone, I hope I'm in love...to just be comfortable."

Dawson's Creek is a dream come true for Katie. "I'd love to do the show for a long time, and I want to pursue a career in film and eventually, maybe theatre," she says. What does it all boil down to? "I just want to work, and I love to work and perform." That's great news, Katie—because we love to watch you!

"I Can Buy Nicer Gifts"

Success hasn't changed Katie very much. "Success," she explains, "is about getting an education and being happy." Her family helps to keep her grounded. With them around there's not much of a chance that Katie will get sucked into the false world of Hollywood. She explains her perspective very simply, saying, "I don't think there's any mark I can make. And if I did think that, my family would knock me over the side of my head, like, 'Who do you think you are?'" So what is she doing now? "I'm taking each day as it comes," she says. "I'm just having fun." Has stardom changed her life at all? "I can buy nicer gifts for people," she says simply. Now that's a star who is very down-to-earth!

Dawson's Creek

Michelle

Joshua

Katie

James

Dawson's Creek

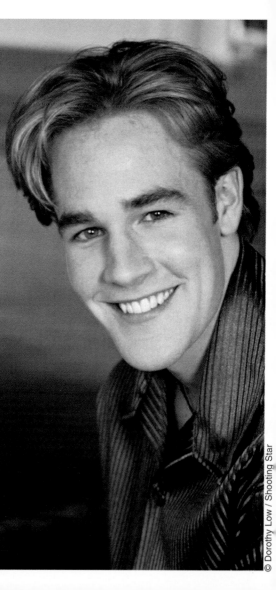

Dawson's Creek

Dawson's Creek

Dawson's Creek

Creek

8

Michelle Williams

Growing Up (and Moving Out!)

Kalispell, Montana, is a town even smaller than Capeside, and is lucky enough to claim Michelle Williams as its own. Michelle was born there, on September 9, 1980, and spent most of her pre-teen years in Kalispell with her father, Larry, a commodities trader, her mother, Carla, a homemaker, and her four younger siblings.

What's Montana like? Well, it's not exactly a spring break destination. "It was wide open, beautiful—and cold!" Michelle says. "One winter, the temperature was lower than 30 below zero every day for over a month." So when Michelle was nine years old the family moved from small town Kalispell to bigger (and warmer!) San Diego.

Even though she was pretty young, Michelle recalls the move like it was yesterday: "I can remember feeling so different...from all the other kids." Michelle uses these outcast-at-school memories when she's trying to get into character on *Dawson's Creek*. "Jen, the character I play, is definitely from a different world than the kids at her new school," Michelle explains. And as we all know, high school can be hard on anyone, but Michelle had a particularly tough time. In fact, she declares that high school was "the most miserable time of my life." Michelle decided she would prefer to be home-schooled and privately tutored after some awful experiences during her freshman year. "[Ninth grade] was so hard for me," she confides. "People really underestimate how tough high school can be for kids...You have to get good grades and look and act a certain way to fit in, and everyone thinks you need a boyfriend." Some kids picked on her, and a couple of girls even beat her up. "There was one girl who used to torture me. She stole my clothes out of my gym locker and hid them," Michelle says. "My personal favorite was the time she sent me a fake note from this very cute boy in my class. It read, 'Meet me by the back stairs at 3.' Of course I felt like a big fool when I showed up and he wasn't there." It's hard to imagine all this when looking at the bright, beautiful, and successful actress today, but things got so bad that Michelle used to spend lunch period hiding in one of the bathroom stalls. "When we go on the set and do the big hallway scenes, I still get sweaty palms," she confesses.

Luckily, Michelle's parents agreed to her plan to be home-schooled. She had joined a local theatre group and started acting shortly after her family moved to San Diego (and gave up her unique dream of becoming the first female heavyweight boxing champion of the world!). Before she knew it, her father was driving her to jobs regularly. Does this remind you a little bit of James Van Der Beek's family? Well, if you thought they were committed to getting his career started, wait till you hear what Michelle's family did for her! In addition to home-schooling her so she could graduate early (and so she could get away from her high school),

Michelle's father would also drive her all the way from San Diego to Los Angeles (a two-hour trip each way) for auditions. Michelle left high school at 15 (after her freshman year), and she graduated the next year at 16. After she graduated, she moved to L.A. in order to concentrate on her career. "I got an apartment, and my parents took turns staying with me," she says. But the family separation was too much for her parents and siblings, and eventually Michelle wound up living on her own. "I know it's crazy," she says. "My mother was scared out of her mind."

This lifestyle has definitely taken a toll, though. Michelle says, "I'm kind of isolated because I don't go to high school. It's a fun conversation piece for ten minutes, then people get bored." And though most kids would jump at the chance to live on their own, Michelle wants you to know that being independent isn't all it's cracked up to be. "I miss my family," she says. "It's really hard to be away from my sister, Paige. She's 14 and doing all these fun things, like going to homecoming." Like Katie, she uses the phone to keep in touch with her family—and to give her sister lots of advice. And while this lifestyle as been stressful at times, it has helped Michelle get some plum roles, too. She has the second–longest resume of any of the actors on *Dawson's Creek*.

From Aliens to Lassie

Michelle was 13 when she landed her first movie role, the part of Young Sil, an alien in the cult film *Species*. It wasn't quite as important a movie to her as it became to its following. To her, "it was just a job. I was a thirteen-year-old going to work and they put stuff on my face." Now, says Michelle, people "send me letters and ask me to come to their alien conventions...they took it as reality."

Her next big role was the character of April in the 1994 movie *Lassie*. The next year, Michelle landed a role in the movie *Timemaster* as Annie. She didn't enjoy making that movie very much. She says that the cast flipped the "M" in *Timemaster* to make it read "TimeWaster" because the shooting just took forever. Her next film, however, was anything but a waste of time. It was her biggest-star-power movie to date, the recent dramatic film *A Thousand Acres*, starring Jessica Lange, Michelle Pfeiffer, Jennifer Jason Leigh and

Jason Robards. Michelle Williams played Michelle Pfeiffer's daughter, Pammy. This movie gave Michelle the chance to work side-by-side with some of Hollywood's biggest and most respected names. When asked what she learned from working with Jessica Lange, Michelle answered, "Grace. Things that I don't think I really realize now. Just immeasurable...but above all, grace." Michelle says however that she learned a lot from each of the actresses. "It was different things from the three of them; with Jessica it was about grace, Michelle is ethereal, Jennifer is so complex. I learned a lot; what I learned cannot be expressed in words," she explains.

In addition to her work in movies, Michelle has appeared in guest spots on several TV shows, including *Step by Step* and *Home Improvement*. She's also appeared in the television movies *A Mother's Justice* and *Killing Mr. Griffin*.

Michelle on Jen

Michelle describes Jen as "an outsider coming to Capeside from a fast-paced New York lifestyle. Ostensibly she's come to help her strict grandmother care for her seriously ailing grandfather, but she's hiding a troubled past. More sophisticated and worldly than the other three teen characters, she's an old soul, having done a lot and grown up fast. I think a part of Jen is really looking to regain her innocence and lead the quintessential teenage life, and she wants to fit in with these more carefree kids. But there's another part of her that still longs for the city lights, taxi rides, bars, and clubs. She made some mistakes, and got sent to Capeside by her parents in hopes that she'd begin to realize she should slow down and change her ways."

Michelle says she can relate to some of these changes. In order to film the show, she had to move across the country from fast-paced L.A. to the much smaller and slower-paced city of Wilmington, North Carolina. "It's quite a change from Los Angeles," Michelle says. "[Wilmington] is beautiful and a nice pace for awhile, but at first it was a strange switch from the city and traffic. Having the experience of moving from a big city to a small town does make it easier to relate to Jen, however."

Michelle bristles at criticism of the show's content—especially concerning Jen's past, and the reasons why her family had her move to

Capeside. "I always imagined that some controversy would arise," she says. "But the issues that we deal with [on the show], while they're called controversial, really are true to life, and they exist. And every teenager, regardless of where they live, their social standing, their class—everyone is going to be going through or feeling these emotions, so why not put it out in the open and give them some basis to go on?" It's no surprise that this open, honest actress asks, "Why not talk about [these issues]?"

But does she agree with critics of the show who have said that the witty, sarcastic exchanges and dialogue of the main characters is unrealistic? Not at all, Michelle emphasizes. "I didn't have access to intelligent dialogue when I was a kid," she relates. "But I wish I could have expressed my feelings this way. These issues and topics are really prevalent."

Life on Location - The Merry Prankster

Michelle, if you're to believe the reports of her castmates, is a bit of a practical joker. The whole cast was staying in the Wilmington Howard Johnson's in May 1997, immediately after they had all arrived for filming. Michelle and Katie thought it would be a good time to pull a little joke on James and Josh. So one day the girls locked the two boys out of their hotel rooms—leaving them standing in the hallway wearing nothing but their boxers. "They didn't want to go into the lobby because they were only in their underwear," says Michelle. "We just terrorized them." What does she have in mind for her next practical joke? Well, she's been talking to the effects crew lately to get some ideas. She's thinking about attaching a metal bar to the underside of Josh's new truck so it will continually emit a clicking noise. "It'll drive him crazy," she says with an impish grin.

Although it can sometimes be a little lonely for the four stars to be on location together away from their families and friends, Michelle says it's a lot of fun, too. "It's like college, like we're all in one big sorority or something," Michelle exudes. "It's just fabulous how we've all gotten along, because we really had no choice...Not knowing anyone else has forced the cast to bond." The four stars often go out to eat together. "They have the best restaurants here [in Wilmington]," says Michelle. "We all have big appetites!"

But Michelle and Katie would probably

choose to spend a lot of time together no matter what their circumstances. The two will often hang out at one of their apartments at the end of a long work day. Part of the reason is that there's not a lot to do in Wilmington: "The nightlife in North Carolina—it's just raging," Michelle jokes. But the two friends also prefer to just kick back and relax. "Katie and I make a point of finding time to goof off and be kids. We also bake cookies and drink a lot of coffee. I'm pretty happy to have a buddy to do girl stuff with."

Every night isn't quiet and relaxing, however. Michelle says the cast is busy getting into "nasty arguments." What about? Are they arguing over who gets the best lines, or who has more lines, things like that? Nope, these guys like to talk about other stuff—like politics, religion, or welfare reform. It can get a little brutal. "But," Michelle says, "we can all hold our own."

Perhaps the actors' passion for reading is the reason they can hold their own. Michelle and Josh have both been described as voracious readers, especially when they're on location. Michelle is often found curled up with a copy of a classic such as Hermann Hesse's *Gertrude* or Dostoyevsky's *Notes From the Underground*. Of all of the fictional characters out there, it's Gertrude, from Hermann Hesse's book, that Michelle would most like to play. Who knows, maybe if *Dawson's Creek* continues to do well, someone will give her the chance. Right now, though, Michelle's being given the chance to work on a very different kind of film.

Upcoming Projects

Michelle will be playing the role of Molly in the soon-to-be-released movie *Halloween:H20*, also known as *Halloween 7: The Revenge of Laurie Strode*. It's a twentieth-anniversary celebration of the release of the original *Halloween* movie. Jamie Lee Curtis will reprise the role of Laurie Strode. Also working on the film, which was filmed in the late winter and early spring of 1998, are Joseph Gordon Levitt from *3rd Rock From the Sun*, Josh Hartnett from *Cracker*, and Charles S. Dutton. Josh Hartnett will be playing Laurie Strode's son. Kevin Williamson came up with the story, Robert Zappia wrote the script, and Steve Miner will be directing the movie.

Dealing With Success

So, how will this early success (Michelle's only 17, after all) affect the rest of her life? "I'll be addicted to heroin and robbing mini-marts in a couple of years, I'm sure," Michelle predicts. As her fans, we're sure that this is another example of this rising young star's terrific sense of humor!

9

Joshua Jackson

Growing Up

With Josh, what you see is what you get. The wittiest cast member of *Dawson's Creek* was born on June 11, 1978 in Vancouver, British Columbia, Canada. He grew up with his mom, Fiona, who is a casting director, and his younger sister, Aisleigh (pronounced "Ashley"). Josh's family was living in Los Angeles when his parents divorced. After the divorce, Josh explains, "It was just me, my sister, and my mother, and we went at it alone." The three of them "gradually moved back up the West Coast." He admits that there were a few rough years during this period. "I went from being a very well-off little kid to having a couple rough years, to rebuilding—my mother did that. She and I are very close."

Josh ended up at Kitsilano High School in Vancouver. He describes it as "an ex-hippie place. It's very liberal." Josh had some problems with school, though. Josh has even gone so far as describing his education as "heinous" (which means really, really bad) and "abbreviated and herky-jerky." Josh ran into enough problems in high school that he didn't actually graduate. He now has a G.E.D. (General Equivalency Degree), which is like a high school diploma, except that it's based on one test, instead of four years of school. Josh isn't happy with it, though. "I've never been more ashamed of myself in my life than when I got to the end of that test and just went, oh, God, I can't believe I just did this." He called the test "farcical," or something of a joke. He's interested in furthering his education—but we'll talk about that later when we see what his future plans are.

There are three other members of Josh's family that we haven't yet mentioned. Josh has a dog named Shumba (which means "lion" in

Swahili—you can see him in the Winter/Spring J. Crew catalogue!), a cat named Magic, and a turtle called Searesha. Shumba is considered the third roommate in Josh and James's apartment because he's so incredibly big (a Labrador/Rottweiler mix).

Josh turned 20 at the end of the pilot season. Because Josh started acting so early it's hard to separate "growing up" from "how he got started." So we'll move on to "how he got started."

How He Got Started, or, How Even the Best Plans Backfire

When Josh was nine years old, he told his mom that he wanted to start acting. His mom, a casting director, didn't think acting was a good choice for her son, and thought that one audition would be enough to discourage Josh. So she brought little Josh to his first professional audition, assuming that it would be his last. It threw a bit of a kink in her plan when he got the part. Soon he was appearing all over America in a series of tourism spots for "Beautiful British Columbia." From there he went on to compile the longest resume of anyone in the *Dawson's Creek* cast. Things certainly haven't turned out the way his mother had hoped—instead of being discouraged from an acting career, Josh had begun something major. So much for that plan!

Josh's next gig was a small part on the TV series *MacGyver*. Since his mom was the casting director, and since the show was filmed in their hometown of Vancouver, this was a pretty convenient role. After that Josh's mom brought him in for a small part in the movie *Crooked Hearts*, starring Peter Berg (from *Chicago Hope*), Vincent D'Onofrio, Noah Wyle (from *E.R.*), Juliette Lewis and "a bunch of others." He got the part, of course. He played Tom, or as he says, "the young Peter Berg." He was only in "the first ten minutes or so" but "Wyle and Berg were very cool and took us out all the time."

The next year, the movie's producer did a play in Seattle. "It was a musical version of *Willy Wonka and the Chocolate Factory* and I played Charlie...The play's casting director, Laura Kennedy, got me hooked up with William Morris as my agent." (Just in case you didn't know, the William Morris Agency is one of the most prestigious talent agencies around.) Six months after that, Josh was again playing Charlie—but this time in *The Mighty Ducks*. Says Josh, "There was a snowball effect after that."

Josh was definitely on a roll. *The Mighty Ducks* came out in 1992. In 1993 Josh played the role of Billy in the film *Digger*, and in 1994 he played Mark Baker in the movie *Andre*. *D2: The Mighty Ducks* also came out 1994 and Josh reprised his role of Charlie Conway. *Magic in the Water*, in which he played Joshua Black, came out in 1995.

In 1996 Josh made two Showtime Contemporary Classics, *Ronnie and Julie*, an updated version of Shakespeare's *Romeo and Juliet*, and *Robin of Locksley*, which is based on the Robin Hood legend. Josh plays Ronnie Monroe (or Romeo) in *Ronnie and Julie*, and John Prince, Jr. in *Robin of Locksley*. Later that year, Josh also filmed *D3: The Mighty Ducks*. The next part Josh landed was Pacey—but we'll talk about that in just a sec.

He got his next part, a small role as a film class student in *Scream 2* through Kevin Williamson. Josh tells about his experiences filming the scene. "It was amazing. One day on the [*Dawson's Creek*] set, Kevin Williamson came up and said, 'Hey, I want to ask you a huge favor. It's OK if you don't want to do this, but I was wondering if you'd be in a scene in

Scream 2.' And I was like, 'Of course!' They flew me to L.A., put me up in a big hotel and gave me a driver and per diem money. I got to meet Neve Campbell—who I have a huge crush on now—Sarah Michelle Gellar and the guys from *Scream 2.* It was great!" Sounds like a pretty cool time!

Becoming Pacey

Josh tried out for *Dawson's Creek* in Los Angeles. He describes getting the role pretty casually: "I just happened to be in L.A. and went in and read for Pacey." The producers called him back the next day and had him read for Dawson. "Then," says Josh, "they said never mind." They didn't *mean* never mind, apparently, because the next day he got a call asking him to come in and read for Pacey again. Overall, he says, the process "took about five days." When he was done with his last reading and on his way out, the producers said, "Hey, by the way, we'll see you in North Carolina." He'd made it!

By the way, when Josh auditioned he asked Kevin Williamson what the deal was with the name Pacey. It turns out that Pacey was the name of one of Kevin's best friends when he was growing up.

Josh on Pacey (or is it Pacey on Josh?)

"Pacey's very abrasive on the surface, but I like to think in the end that he's redeemable," Josh says. "I think he clings so hard to Dawson because he's the only person Pacey can really hang out with and be who he wants to be." As for whether or not the two are at all alike, Josh answers, "We're exactly the same. I was that guy at 15, and I am that guy now. I haven't been acting for the last six months; I've just been showing up and being myself." Hey, that sounds like a great gig!

And no, Josh doesn't want to be Dawson. "Yes, I could have [played the part]. But I wouldn't have brought the same things to the part that [James Van Der Beek] does. So the short answer is no, and the long answer is yes, I could have, but you wouldn't be enjoying the show as much."

Pacey and Tamara: Controversial Couple

The questions everyone has been asking (other than whether Joey and Dawson will get together) is what Josh thought of the Pacey/Tamara relationship, and what it was like to kiss an older woman. Josh seems to have pretty positive views of both. When he found out about the plot line he was in quite a hurry to tell his friends back in British Columbia. "I called them up and said, 'Man, you'll never believe what I get to do on this show!'" he says. Has he ever been involved with any of his teachers? "Unfortunately, I didn't have the pleasure of an illicit affair with a stunning English teacher." (Hmm, it's odd that he only included English teachers—and stunning English teachers at that. Are you thinking what I'm thinking?) Josh adds, though, that "if any English teachers want to come forward now...If Mrs. Stopple's out there," he'd be ready to renew acquaintances! And if you're wondering what it's like to kiss a woman twice your age, Josh has the answer for you. "It's kind of like kissing a woman the same age as you—nice." And no, he did not feel like he was kissing his mother. "No slight against my mother—I love ya, Mom—but Leann [Leann Hunley plays Tamara] is a beautiful woman, and my mother is...my mother." Josh admits to not getting the kiss right on the first take. "I had to do a lot of takes on that, I wanted to make sure it was exactly right." (Yeah, sure, it sounds very...professional of him.) Leann, though, "was very cool about it. I was impressed by how graceful she was with it."

So basically, everyone just felt "nice" about the Pacey/Tamara scenes? Well, Leann "was having pangs of guilt because of the real-life teacher/student coupling." Other than that, they all seem to have enjoyed themselves...a lot!

At a news conference for the show, Josh discussed some of the issues involved in Pacey's and Tamara's relationship. Several people brought up the Seattle case in the news recently where a teacher had a relationship with, and later had the child of, one of her thirteen-year-old students. Josh is quick to dismiss any comparisons between the two stories. "I don't want to draw a parallel between what happened in Seattle and what happens on the show. I saw that Seattle woman interviewed on TV and she's got a couple of screws loose and the kid didn't know what he was doing." How is the Pacey/Tamara story any different? "My character is a little bit older," he says. "Pacey is the pursuer and instead of the teacher being all for, she's deadly against. She's having an obvious crisis of conscience and is aware of doing something she thinks is wrong but is unable to hold back. Inevitably, she is punished for it." He goes on to say, "Pacey doesn't think he's gonna get her. She flirts with him and he thinks it's cool. When it works out, he's not only trying to seduce her, he's in love. After that first kiss, it's all over."

Josh believes that "open communication is the best way to deal with sex. If you've got a problem and you believe your children to be too young to enter into the sexual ballgame, talk to them." He applies this advice to his own life, too. "My fourteen-year-old sister is getting into the dating game now and it's uncomfortable, but I do it." He still admits that at times, "it's uncomfortable as hell."

Josh is thrilled to be working on a show that he feels deals with teen issues in a realistic way. "I've seen *My So-Called Life* a couple of times, and I think that was a good show," Josh says, "but there were no happy times—it was always some sort of melodrama. I hope that's the difference with our show. Teendom is tough...but there are happy times, too. Life has to be good sometimes, or else we might as well all do a lemming leap."

Probing his Personal Life

When looking over all of the things Josh has said about dating, the first word to come to mind is not "selective" or "choosy." Quite the opposite in fact. Josh has told people that he's looking for "a girl with a pulse." When asked what actress he'd like to kiss he said, "Most anybody's who's worked in the last decade." And yes, he's more than willing to go out with a non-actress. "If I only dated actresses, I'd be a very lonely man." He's certainly leaving his options open. And no, he's not dating Katie Holmes, although he teases, "Oh, yeah. I'm dating Katie, Michelle, and Jimmy—the whole cast." And don't try to get him to choose between Michelle and Katie—he'll choose both!

You might be surprised to find out that he considers himself pretty clumsy with girls—though if Pacey's pick-up line at the bar is any indication of Josh's lines (Pacey asks a girl for a quarter to call God and tell him one of his angels is missing), you might not be that surprised. In terms of music, Josh goes in for blues/jazz mostly, but "as for contemporary music, I listen to rap. I like Common Sense. *Resurrection* is probably the best hip-hop album of all time." Oh, and he also wears boxers, not briefs. "Briefs just aren't comfortable—nothing personal to all you brief wearers out there."

Like the other stars of the show, Josh enjoys spending time with his castmates. "We're like a family, and I think that plays into the show," he explains. "It helps to be friendly off-camera, so when you're on camera, you have that dynamic, too. I think that's really nice."

Upcoming Projects

Josh will be appearing in two films that are scheduled for release in 1998. The first, *Apt Pupil*, is an adaptation of Stephen King's short story by the same name. It stars Brad Renfro and Ian McKellan. Josh plays Brad Renfro's best friend. He describes the movie as "very disturbing—just really dark, dark stuff." The second upcoming movie is *Wild River*, in which he plays Sylvester. He hasn't worked on any projects since wrapping up the filming of *Dawson's Creek*, though. He's currently "gainfully unemployed" and not overly upset about it.

Future Plans

Most of Josh's future plans involve going to college. He once wanted to be archaeologist, then decided he wanted to be an architect. "It only dawned on me lately that I could have a career as an actor. But I'll go to school after the show and figure out what I want to do with the rest of my life." He knows what he really wants to get out of college—not grades (like Pacey, he's "not a grades-oriented person")—but exchanges of ideas. "I can read all the books I want, but I can only think with one mind and I don't have access to a bunch of different people who are tackling the exact same circumstances that I'm tackling, and I just—I can't wait." He admits that he might be building it up a little too much, but says, "I can't wait to dive in there and do stuff like that."

His mom would like him to go to college now, but she understands that Hollywood doesn't wait for people. Josh describes his mom as being "pleased as punch that I'm getting to do something that I enjoy." The best part of it, though, is that "it's setting me up to do whatever I want for the rest of my life."

Josh doesn't have any plans to be in a *The Mighty Ducks 4*, if Disney decides to make one. He figures "they'd bring in younger kids—our cute factor is running out." Josh would also "love to do a guest appearance on the *X-Files*. It's filmed right there in Vancouver. I've wanted to be on it for five years, I've tried to get on it, I've asked to get on it. But I think the effort is doomed." (Sounds like James and his commercials, doesn't it?) Most of all, he hopes "to enjoy success and be able to do all I want as an actor. And to just keep getting better."

Publicity up the Wazoo

He saw the first promo commercials for *Dawson's Creek* in North Carolina and thought they were pretty good. He was in New Orleans for the premiere with the rest of the cast (except Katie) "promoting ourselves shamelessly" at an important television convention. Then he and James were flown in to New York City for a *Seventeen* magazine function and had an entire audience (of girls, we can assume) "screaming for the sake of screaming." They did an *Entertainment Weekly* photo shoot "wearing this $2,000 suit...the nicest piece of clothing I will ever wear." The show's publicist brags about Josh reading the works of John Locke (a heavy-duty, died-a-long-time-ago philosopher—not exactly beach reading!). So far, Josh has gotten two marriage proposals from young girls in Japan who "expressed their desire to have my hand in holy matrimony." He says that "if I see my face on a poster one more time, I'm probably going to be ill." Overall, he rates the publicity experience "bizarre" and "surreal." (Have you noticed how often those words come up in conversations with all the actors?) As wild a ride as it must be, Josh is thrilled to have had it. "It showed how behind the show the WB is. It was good to get people in the door, now we have to keep 'em there." Don't worry, Josh-we're not going anywhere!

Playing Around and (Gasp!) Working on Location

"I know this is really gonna shock you all, but I'm a practical joker." Consider us shocked! Josh considers himself a serious, high-level prankster. "I've seen that boy's butt more times than I care to say," says co-star Michelle. Josh has played a couple of pranks on the grips and electrical guys, two groups of people most actors try not to get on the bad side of. It came back to him during the filming of "The Breakfast Club" episode, though. "In "The Breakfast Club" episode," Josh explains, "we run through the hall, and I'm supposed to come crashing through a door, but the grips had locked the door on me, and we did, like, a Three Stooges thing with all of us like dominoes hitting the door." Ouch! That must have hurt! "After I woke up from my concussion, I thought it was really funny," he kids.

He's enjoying being in Wilmington, too. "Wilmington in the summer is like a resort. After you wrap, you put on the swim trunks and go jump into the ocean." Unfortunately they don't just shoot in the summer, and "in the winter, it's a little different," hesitates Josh. "If I wasn't working, I don't know what I'd do. I can't go to clubs because I'm not old enough." He quickly adds, "It's a beautiful town, but I'm glad to be working while I'm there."

Josh says his biggest challenge on the show is trying to be funny. With a sense of humor as quick as his, it's hard to believe Josh feels like he has to work at it. He finds the acting fairly easy, mostly due to the quality of the writing, but also because he's already so much like Pacey. He explains that "if it was poorly written or if I had to struggle with it, I don't know, maybe it would be difficult, but because we have good writers who are putting thought into the dialogue, into the actions that we're putting on screen, my job becomes so easy. I just basically have to show up and know the words that they've written for me and I'm golden." So what about the show is hard? He says, "Just adapting myself to working these hours and learning how to contain my energy so that I'm awake by the time I get to the end of the day." Why does he need to work on containing his energy? "'Cause I'm generally a fairly boisterous guy." What a surprise, huh?

Josh enjoys rooming with James in Wilmington, along with Josh's dog (the one from the J. Crew catalogue, remember?) He says that the rest of the cast is "really tight." After nearly six months on the set Josh reports that they've become a lot like brothers and sisters. "There are fights and squabbles, ups and downs, but we get along really well."

Brat Packers and Joe, the Guy Who Fixes Your Plumbing

A lot of people have asked Josh which of the Brat Packers he thinks he's most like—Rob Lowe, Emilio Estevez, Anthony Michael Hall, Judd Nelson, or Andrew McCarthy. His usual answer? "I feel like a multi-Brat-Packer. I channel their spirits though me." So what does he think about the comparisons to the Brat Pack? "I've never minded being compared to anybody, you know. I mean if you want to—that's actually a funny comparison, like Emilio Estevez would get a kick out of me being compared to him 10 years ago. But being compared to the Brat Pack, that's not a problem. The Brat Pack were successful actors and they made good movies and seminal movies that marked their age. So I have no problem being compared to someone—I mean especially if I'm being compared to someone successful. Sure. Compare away. It doesn't bother me. You know, people are always like, man, I don't like being compared to so and so. You want to compare me to the Brat Pack, feel free, I mean I don't have a problem with that." He does have one caveat: "If you want to compare me to Joe, the guy who fixes your plumbing, that might be a different story."

Dizzying Change or Same Old-Same Old?

Pretty much the same old, same old, according to Josh. He's still not widely recognized, although a woman at the Department of Motor Vehicles did give him his license plate for free because she'd seen him in *The Mighty Ducks* movies. Josh isn't going on a spending spree, though, he has rented a new Chevy Tahoe (the one Michelle wants to attach the noise bar to). And when asked if all of this attention has changed him from a nice Canadian boy, Josh dismisses it by saying, "Unfortunately, I was never a nice Canadian boy."

You've got to admit, the guy can make you laugh!

10

Kevin Williamson

No book about Dawson's Creek would be complete without discussing Kevin Williamson, the creator of the show. Right now, he's about as hot as a director/producer/writer can get. After his successes with *Scream*, *Scream 2*, and *I Know What You Did Last Summer*, Kevin is the guy everyone wants to work with.

Which may be why he's currently working on five different projects. Yes, five. In one year, Kevin launched *Dawson's Creek*, filmed *Killing Mrs. Tingle*, came up with the story for *Halloween 7*, and developed the script for

Scream 3. In addition to these projects, which are enough to keep anyone busy, he's working on scripts for two other films — one an action movie, and the other a romantic comedy. Has this guy cloned himself, or what?

No. Here's how he deals with all the work and stress: "I'm having a nervous breakdown," he says. "My assistant was proofing a script the other day, and she went, 'Kevin, who's Luke?' and I realized I was writing the wrong character in the wrong plot." That's busy! But someone whose goal is "to do for action movies what *Scream* did for horror movies," or, as he says later, "to kick its butt," can't afford to take much time off. Especially when he's still kicking butt in the genres he's already attacked.

He's come a long way since he was born in New Bern, North Carolina, a little over 30 years ago. As a teenager, Kevin was an avid reader and an absolute movie freak — a lot like Dawson. In fact, Dawson's character is based on Kevin's teenage self, and Joey is based on his best friend, Fanny Norwood.

It's easy to see where Dawson comes from when you listen to Kevin talk. "When I was a kid, I wanted life to be like the movies. When you kissed the girl, it was supposed to be the sun setting on the beach, a John Williams score in the background and this windswept beauty in your arms." Sounds a lot like Dawson, doesn't it?

Kevin wrote, directed, and produced films when he was a kid, too, starting at the age of 11 with the thriller *White as a Ghost*. Like Dawson, he featured his friends as the stars of the film—in fact his next-door neighbor had to play both the murderer and the victim. (That must have involved some splicing and dicing!)

The character of Joey is pretty true to life, too. Her background (mother dead, father in jail, etc.) is made-up, but "Fanny contributed a great deal to Joey's characterization and Joey is very much Fanny." And for all of you Joey-Dawson romantics out there, you'll be pleased to know that Joey's relationship with Dawson is based primarily on Williamson's relationship with Fanny—and that the two ended up dating. They're not together now, though, having lost track of each other for several years until Fanny read about the series and gave Williamson a call. (More about that later!)

Williamson gets a lot of praise for his realistic—and very frank—dialogue. But it's the frankness that has also gotten him into trouble with some critics of *Dawson's Creek*. These critics have said that there's just too much sex on the show, which is intended for a teenager-and-older audience. Kevin isn't bothered by this criticism, though. "[These kids] may talk big, but look at their behavior. If you really watch what's happening on the show, it's about this young boy who wants to hold this girl's hand at the movies." To him, *Dawson's Creek* is the story of "how kids really act now and how I wish I had acted 15 years ago." Like when you think of the perfect response to a put-down two hours after you could have used it, Kevin writes his stories the way he wishes he could have done when he was experiencing them. "It's my childhood come to life," he says, "but now I get to go back to these places and create these situations where I can change the ending and have it turn out like I wish it would have." Wouldn't it be nice if we could all do that (and do it as well as he does)?

11

The First Season

Here's a handy reference to the episodes from the first season of Dawson's Creek.

Pilot-Emotions in Motion

Dawson Leery and Josephine "Joey" Potter begin their sophomore year at Capeside High School struggling with the knowledge that their lifelong friendship may be threatened and forever changed by "hormones" and other factors. The arrival of the mysterious and beautiful Jennifer Lindley adds to their confusion, as the big-city girl enchants Dawson and bothers Joey. Finally, longtime buddy Pacey Witter fumbles his way into an adult situation with a woman who turns out to be his English teacher.

Episode #101-Dirty Dancing

Dawson writes Jen into his movie, much to Joey's disdain. At school, Dawson wheedles his way into a film class but is disappointed to discover that football-star Cliff has scripted a movie about his athletic talent. Jen later accepts Cliff's offer to go to the school dance together, at which Dawson makes a scene, causing Jen to walk out. Joey confronts Mrs. Leery after overhearing her on the phone with her co-anchor, and Pacey's relentless pursuit of Ms. Jacobs pays off with a first kiss.

Episode #102-A Prelude to a Kiss

Dawson manages to finagle himself a spot in the film class at Capeside High School, but only under the condition that he remain a silent observer. His relationship with Jen has progressed enough that Dawson dreams of a perfect first kiss with her; however, these plans go awry when Jen sees something that distracts her from their romantic moment. Meanwhile, Joey is swept off her feet by a handsome rich guy, Anderson Crawford, and also witnesses Mrs. Leery in a compromising position with another man. Finally, Pacey and Ms. Jacobs have a secret rendezvous that turns out to be not-so-secret after all.

Episode #103-Carnal Knowledge

Dawson sees his mother kissing another man on the day of his parent's twentieth anniversary. Looking to Joey for support, Dawson discovers that she has been aware of the affair and feels betrayed by his best friend. Further troubles come to Dawson as Jen reveals her dark past and the real reasons why she is living in Capeside. Pacey and Ms. Jacobs continue to grow closer, but are understandably upset when Pacey discovers that Dawson has accidentally videotaped them.

Episode #104-Blown Away

As Capeside prepares for a terrible hurricane that's about to hit, Jen's and Joey's families wind up seeking shelter at the Leery's house. Tempers flare everywhere: Dawson confronts his mother about her affair and she in turn confesses to both him and his father; Jen's grandmother exchanges acrimonious words with Joey's pregnant sister, Bessie, and her boyfriend, Bodie, about their unborn child; and Pacey and his older brother, Deputy Doug Witter, are bitter rivals for Ms. Jacob's affections as they weather out the storm at the teacher's beach house.

Episode #105-Look Who's Talking

With Bodie out of town on a business trip, Bessie goes into labor early and is forced to wait at Dawson's house for an ambulance. Jen deals with her religious differences with her grandmother, whose nursing skills help Bessie through a difficult labor. However, Bessie's cries of pain bring back terrible memories for Joey of her mother's death from cancer, and she seeks comfort from Dawson. Pacey and Ms. Jacobs are forced to confront rumors about their relationship that come to the attention of the school board, which puts a sudden end to their affair as Ms. Jacobs resigns and moves away from Capeside.

Episode #106-The Breakfast Club

In this take-off of the classic movie featuring the Brat Pack, the four friends are stuck together in Saturday detention under the watchful eye of the school librarian. With the school troublemaker stirring things up, the kids play a game of Truth or Dare that has startling consequences.

Episode #107-Escape from New York

Billy, Jen's ex-boyfriend from New York, shows up at Capeside with the intention of winning back her affections. Much to Dawson's dismay, Jen seems receptive to Billy's overtures. Pacey convinces Joey, who is tired and depressed from working and taking care of her new nephew, into going to a beach party with him. Unfortunately, Joey drinks too much and Pacey has to carry her home, where she sleepily and drunkenly kisses Dawson.

Episode #108-In the Company of Men

Dawson is majorly bummed after his breakup with Jen. Billy, back in town again, offers just the distraction Dawson is looking for, taking Dawson and Pacey to a bar in Providence, Rhode Island to pick up chicks. Dawson hits it off with a nice (slightly older!) woman who invites him back to her place as a way of showing off to his friends. Dawson turns down the offer because he realizes he's still hung up on Jen. Arriving home in the wee hours of the morning, Dawson finds Joey in his room. He crashes with her, asking if she can wait until later to discuss his adventure. As he drifts off to sleep, Joey tells him she can wait.

Episode #109-Modern Romance

Dawson becomes jealous over Jen's decision to go on a date with Cliff, Capeside's star athlete, and masterminds a way to stay close to her by double dating. Meanwhile, Pacey and Joey start to see each other in a new and different way. After Pacey confides these feelings to Dawson, Dawson is forced to confront his own feelings about his best friend, Joey.

Episode #110-Friday the 13th

On Friday the 13th, Dawson holds a séance and revels in frightening practical jokes. As news hits Capeside that young women are being brutally murdered, Jen worries that she might be the next victim after she gets a terrifying phone call. And Pacey befriends a strange young woman, who, unbeknownst to her, is being stalked.

Episode #111-Pretty Woman

When Joey enters a local beauty pageant to earn money towards college, she suddenly finds herself the center of male attention. On the eve of the competition, Dawson is confused as ever when Jen confesses she has some regrets about ending their relationship and Joey unburdens her heart. Meanwhile, the always-contentious Pacey also enters the competition, throwing the judges into an uproar.

Episode #112-Breaking Away

In the first season finale, Dawson finds out that Joey might leave Capeside for an opportunity to study abroad, and the two lifelong friends are forced to face up to their true feelings about each other. Jen and her grandmother try to resolve their religious differences as a death in the family brings them closer together.

12

What's the Buzz?

Pressure, Pressure

The word was out on *Dawson's Creek* weeks before the first episode aired on January 20, 1998. With enticing promotional spots, billboards, and print ads appearing everywhere, teens and adults alike were ready to tune in. To the pleasant surprise of the WB network, the pilot show had an audience of over five million people, rating ahead of the WB's other success, *Buffy the Vampire Slayer*.

It's obvious that the WB has placed a tremendous amount of faith in *Dawson's Creek*. (And who can blame them?!) The WB presented

Kevin Williamson and the stars of the show at an important meeting of the Television Critics Association in July of 1997, before the show even had an official premiere date. The young network believes that *Dawson's Creek* can put them on the map, just the way *Beverly Hills 90210* did for the Fox network almost a decade ago. Interestingly, it's the powerful and committed teen audience that is critical to the success of these shows, and therefore, the entire network.

The *Dawson's Creek* gang was in New Orleans for a huge convention of television affiliates when the first show aired. Although it was a wild experience for the three stars in attendance (Katie Holmes was in Vancouver working on a film), they all managed to take it in stride. How did they deal with the pressure of being the latest-greatest-coolest-hottest thing? No problem, says Josh: "Personally, I don't feel any pressure, because we're already done filming, so it's out of my hands now."

But when the cast and crew returns to film the second season, the pressure will indeed be on. Even during the first season, the cast and crew were big hits in the city of Wilmington. Says Michelle, "We've already started to feel [attention] a little in North Carolina, because it's such a small town...We're mobbed by locals who had a cousin who was an extra on the show." And with more and more people watching each week, the stars will need to learn how to deal with increasing public scrutiny.

"I think we've all tried to immunize ourselves against all the hype because it can be really destructive," Michelle says. "It's been such a barrage of press that I don't think we have any choice but to become used to it," she adds. "How do you prepare yourself for something like that? They don't give you a guidebook or anything." Although the stars say they realized that they were taking part in a special experience, that *Dawson's Creek* wasn't just another show, no one was prepared for the onslaught of attention—both positive and negative.

Rave Reviews

You could probably hear a big collective sigh of relief from WB network executives clear across the country as fabulous reviews started pouring in from newspapers all across the country for the Creek. Here's just a few of the many positive things television critics had to say:

"The acting is great." *New York Newsday*

"This series...is pure soap, redeemed by intelligence and sharp writing." *New York Times*

"The particular appeal lies in the central cast, which contains young, bright break-out talent (all four)." *The Hollywood Reporter*

"...this hour is prime time's closest thing to a contemporary *Catcher in the Rye*." *TV Guide*

"With its attractive cast and adult dialogue, Dawson's Creek has clearly created a beguiling picture of teen life." *Los Angeles Times*

"Holmes...is so perfect that you find yourself wondering why Winona Ryder hasn't just shrugged and gone into real estate." *Village Voice*

And then of course...

We've already discussed some of the controversy and criticism of the Creek. Kevin Williamson himself was pretty surprised at the reaction of the television critics at the July, 1997 meeting. In fact, Kevin was originally told that his story was too tame. "When I first turned the script in to my agent, [he] thought it was too soft and read too much like *Little House on the Prairie*. I was completely shocked," Kevin says. "[So] I was walking into this thing thinking, 'Oh, my God, how do I edge it up?'" But Kevin calmly told the crowd of critics that the plot lines involving Pacey's affair with his teacher, and Joey's habit of sleeping over in Dawson's room seemed believable to him because they had in fact happened to him, or to people he knew.

Fanny Norwood, Kevin's childhood friend upon whom he based the character of Joey, agrees that Kevin's depictions are right on target, although, "I never climbed onto the roof. I just walked right through the front door." And did Fanny's parents have any objections to her sleeping over at Kevin's house? "I told my parents that part was fictionalized," she relates.

WB officials claim that it was not their intention for *Dawson's Creek* to be such a controversial show. "Do I feel we've acted responsibly? Absolutely," says WB chief executive Jamie Kellner. He points out that *Dawson's Creek* is intended for mature audiences, and that many adults enjoy the program. And let's face it—teenagers and their surging hormones have been the basis for thousands of great stories, from *Romeo and Juliet* to *Titanic*.

One in Three Teens Recommends the Creek...

It's the teens that are fueling the success of the show, however. Both guys and girls are tuning in and obsessing over all the characters and plot twists, and the network's advertisers have responded. For the first time, in its short history, the WB network has a program on which advertisers are willing to pay more than $100,000 for a 30-second commercial. In fact, the season finale of *Dawson's Creek* on May 19, 1998 commanded $225,000 and up for each commercial! And the pairing of *Dawson's Creek* with *Buffy the Vampire Slayer* has made Tuesday nights on the WB has become *the* place to be.

13

Test Your Knowledge

Now that you've read all the inside info on the Creek, it's time for a little test. See how well you can do on these questions. All of the answers are in this book. (You can check your answers at the end of the chapter.)

1. What's the name of the town *Dawson's Creek* is filmed in?
   a) Wilmington, Vermont
   b) Wilmington, Delaware
   c) Wilmington, North Carolina
   d) Wilmington, Indiana

2. What's the name of the town *Dawson's Creek* is set in?
   a) Bayside
   b) Capeside
   c) Seaside
   d) Shoreside
3. Who plays Jen Lindley, Dawson's love interest?
   a) Neve Campbell
   b) Katie Holmes
   c) Sarah Michelle Gellar
   d) Michelle Williams
4. What's the name of the teacher with whom Josh Jackson's character has an affair?
   a) Pamela
   b) Tamara
   c) Katie
   d) Mrs. Leery
5. Which of the actors grew up in Toledo, Ohio?
   a) Michelle Williams
   b) Josh Jackson
   c) James Van Der Beek
   d) Katie Holmes

6. Which character on the show works at the S.S. Icehouse?
   a) Jen Lindley
   b) Joey Potter
   c) Dawson Leery
   d) Pacey Witter
7. What's the name of the producer of *Helmets of Glory?*
   a) Cliff
   b) Dawson Leery
   c) Nellie Olsen
   d) Mr. Gold
8. What did Joey do that landed her in Saturday detention?
   a) punch a football player
   b) talk back to a teacher
   c) throw a basketball in Pacey's face
   d) get too many tardies
9. What was the name of James Van Der Beek's first play?
   a) *Finding the Sun*
   b) *Grease*
   c) *My Marriage To Ernest Borgnine*
   d) *Damn Yankees*

10. Which actor got started in tourism commercials for British Columbia?
    a) James Van Der Beek
    b) Katie Holmes
    c) Michelle Williams
    d) Joshua Jackson

11. What was the name of the character Katie Holmes played in *The Ice Storm*?
    a) Tobey Maguire
    b) Colleen McDonald
    c) Libbets Casey
    d) Josephine Jones

12. What force of nature hits town when Mrs. Leery confesses her affair to Mr. Leery and Dawson?
    a) a tornado
    b) a tidal wave
    c) a hurricane
    d) an earthquake

13. Which of the actors has a small role as a film class student in a scene in *Scream 2*?
    a) James Van Der Beek
    b) Katie Holmes
    c) Michelle Williams
    d) Joshua Jackson

14. What character lives with "Grams"?
    a) Dawson Leery
    b) Joey Potter
    c) Jen Lindley
    d) Pacey Witter
15. Which actor jokes that they'll be "robbing mini-marts" within a couple of years?
    a) James Van Der Beek
    b) Katie Holmes
    c) Michelle Williams
    d) Joshua Jackson
16. What is the name of Josh Jackson's dog?
    a) Magic
    b) Puff
    c) Shamrock
    d) Shumba
17. What does James Van Der Beek's mother run?
    a) marathons
    b) a gymnastics studio
    c) windsprints
    d) a dance hall

18. What team did James Van Der Beek's father pitch for?
    a) the Mets
    b) the Cardinals
    c) the Dodgers
    d) the Orioles
19. Which actor left high school early to be home-schooled and concentrate on acting?
    a) James Van Der Beek
    b) Katie Holmes
    c) Michelle Williams
    d) Joshua Jackson
20. Which of the actors has gone to college?
    a) James Van Der Beek
    b) Katie Holmes
    c) Michelle Williams
    d) Joshua Jackson

14

Rockin' on the Creek

One of the best parts of Dawson's Creek is the amazing selection of tunes that are played each week. It's great the names of some of the artists and their CD's are flashed on the screen at the end of each show, too. Here's a more complete list, though, just in case you haven't been able to find that cool song that's been going through your head.

"A Lot Like You" Colony
"All I Want" Susanna Hoffs
"Always" Sophie Zelmani
"Am I Cool" Nowhere Blossoms
"Amnesia" Toad the Wet Sprocket

"As I Lay Me Down" Sophie B. Hawkins
"Beautiful Thing" Kyf Brewer
"But You" Paul Chiten
"Dammit" Blink 182
"Elegantly Wasted" INXS
"Evaporated" Ben Folds Five
"First Time" Billie Myers
"Flames of Truth" Sarah Masen
"Full of Grace" Sarah McLachlan
"Good Mother" Jann Arden
"Green Apples" Chantal Kreviazuk
"Happiness" Abra Moore
"Healing Hands" Mark Cohn
"Hey, Pretty Girl" BoDeans
"I'm Not Sleeping" Nowhere Blossoms
"I Don't Want to Wait" Paula Cole
"I Know" Barenaked Ladies
"i want you" savage garden
"I'll Stand by You" The Pretenders
"Insecuriousity" Andrew Dorff
"It's the End of the World as We Know It" R.E.M.
"Kingdom" The Slugs
"Mercy Me" Say-So
"Pretty Deep" Tanya Donelly
"Requim" The Slugs
"Right Today" Swerve

"Saturday" Colony
"Seven Shades of Blue" Beth Nielsen Chapman
"Sitting on Top of the World" Amanda Marshall
"Stupid" Chicken Pox
"That's What Love Can Do" Tom Snow
"The Right Place" Eddi Reader
"Thinking Out Loud" Ron Sexsmith
"Too Many Times" Wake Ooloo
"Top of Morning" Hang-Ups
"Touch, Peel and Stand" Days of the New
"truly, madly, deeply" savage garden
"Tubthumping" Chumbawamba
"we are the supercool" Space Monkeys
"We'll Get Through" The Slugs
"What Would Happen" Meredith Brooks
"Will Tomorrow Ever Come?" Dance Hall Crashers
"World Outside" Devlins
"You Don't Know Me" Jann Arden
"Your Pleasure's Mine" Super Deluxe

15

Hot Sites for Cool Info

There are a ton of cool sites on the 'Net for *Dawson's Creek* fans. There are two official sites (they're listed first below) and at least a hundred unofficial sites set up by fans. Visit these sites and you'll find still shots, video clips, interviews, bios, quotes from the shows, episode guides, and much more. Some of the best sites are listed below. Have fun checking them out!

The Official Sites:
• Official Web Site for the show-
 http://www.dawsons-creek.com/
• Official Columbia Tri-Star Site -
http://www.spe.sony.com/tv/shows/dawson/

Dawson's Creek Mailing Lists:

Send an e-mail request to
dawsons_creek@hotmail.com
and make sure to write "subscribe" in the
subject field.
Send an e-mail request to
dawsons-s@canbbs.net
and you should get a reply in one to two hours.

Cool Sites:

• E! Online-
http://www.eonline.com/Hot/Features/Dawson/
index.html?NL3.2
• Ultimate TV's list of Dawson's Creek web-
sites-
http://www.ultimateTV.com/UTVL/utl.html?card+2838
• As the Creek Flows -
http://members.aol.com/Tirakusi/dcreek.html
A good site with a nice page of episode quotes.
• The Unofficial Dawson's Creek Site -
http://members.aol.com/iluvfmuldr/Dawson/main.html
One of the best Creek sites on the net—beauti-
fully displayed, lots of great info. The main
page plays a looping clip of the theme song.
• Dawson's Creek -
http://pc2.simplenet.com/main2.html

A nice site, with icons and backgrounds to download, as well as a RealPlayer version of the entire theme song.

• Totally Teen TV -
http://www.totalTV.com/teen/tn007daw_creek.html
Nice article on the Creek, good interviews with the cast, along with links to some of the best Creek sites.

• The Daily Faith -
http://pages.prodigy.com/faith/dawsons.htm
Check out these articles on Dawson's Creek.

• Creek -
http://dawson.purdueonline.com/creek.html
Good overall DC site.

• TV Guide: Dawson's Creek -
http://www.TVgen.com/TV/magazine/980302/ftr1a.htm
Text and pictures from the March 7, 1998 issue of TV Guide, which featured four different covers—one for each star of the Creek.

• Katie Holmes -
http://www.geocities.com/Hollywood/Studio/8617/katieh.html
Pictures and articles of Katie.

Snail Mail

Here's how to send a letter to one (or more!) of the
stars of the Creek:

Actor's Name
c/o Dawson's Creek
The Warner Brothers Television Network
4000 Warner Blvd.
Burbank, CA 91522

And if you'd like a transcript of one of the shows,
write to:

Transcripts
c/o Dawson's Creek

at the same address as above.

Dawson's Creek Cast:

Dawson Leery	James Van Der Beek
Joey Potter	Katie Holmes
Jennifer Lindley	Michelle Williams
Pacey Witter	Joshua Jackson
Mitch Leery	John Wesley Shipp
Gail Leery	Mary-Margaret Humes
Bessie Potter	Nina Repeta
Bodie	Obi Nfedo
Grams	Mary Beth Peil
Tamara Jacobs	Leann Hunley
Doug Witter	Dylan Neal

Created by:	Kevin Williamson
Executive Producers:	Kevin Williamson
	Paul Stupin
	Charles Rosin
Music Supervisor:	John McCullough
Production Designer:	John "J.T." Walker

About the Author

Hilary Rice is 17 years old and lives with her family outside of Washington, D.C. She will be attending Swarthmore College and plans to major in theater and English literature. *The Stars of Dawson's Creek* is her first published work.